MW00564420

Power Isotonics

Exercise

Bible

Power Isotonics

Exercise Bible

The Best self resistance workouts to build muscle, increase strength, burn fat and sculpt the best body without the use of weights!

Introduction by Marlon Birch C.S.C.S.,

Power Isotonics was written to help you get closer to your physical potential when it comes to real muscle sculpting strengthening exercises. The exercises and routines in this book are quite demanding, so consult your physician and have a physical exam taken prior to the start of this exercise program. Proceed with the suggested exercises and information at your own risk. The publishers and author shall not be liable or responsible for any loss, injury, or damage allegedly arising from the information or suggestions in this book.

Power Isotonics Exercise Bible
Bodybuilding Course

By

Birch Tree Publishing
Published by Birch Tree Publishing

Power Isotonics Exercise Bible
published in 2017, All rights reserved,
No part of this book may be reproduced, scanned,
or distributed in any printed or electronic form without permission.

© 2017 Copyright Birch Tree Publishing
Brought to you by the
Publishers of Birch Tree Publishing
ISBN-978-1-927558-59-1

Birch Tree Publishing

Dedication

To all the people that claim self-resistance does not work and they need to lift weights. Sorry, but after myself and millions of others who received results, you cannot use that excuse again.

Contents

INTRODUCTION
By Marlon Birch,
Natural Pro Bodybuilder and author of Beyond Self Resistance

The world's greatest workout method is now in the palms of your hands.

Few people in the history of bodybuilding have inspired more people than the legendary Charles Atlas. In this book is the same system I used to enhance my physique and developed me into the first ever non-apparatus bodybuilder that used this system of exercise to develop a muscular build and procured two Natural Pro Cards as a natural bodybuilder.

The mainstay of the greats, Atlas, Liederman, and Macfadden, training systems are the very same exercises that are featured in this book (although Charles Atlas called them Dynamic Tension). They are Self Resistance Isotonic-bodybuilding exercises, this is where one muscle group resists the other to create muscle tension to coax muscle growth.

However, these simple exercises can be quite taxing for even the strongest guy. I've personally practiced these exercises my entire life and this system requires no weights, no equipment and can be performed at any point, seated, standing, or lying in bed. These exercises can be done at any time and anywhere, which makes this training system perfect for creating and enhancing a ripped muscular body without weights or machines.

These Isotonic exercises are perfect for increasing tension within the muscles to promote a muscle-growth producing effect. Charles Atlas literally became a living trademark. Although he was a popular and instantly recognizable public figure to five generations of Americans. Atlas passed away in December 1972 at the age of 80. Charles Atlas, a poor immigrant who fought his way from obscurity to reach the very pinnacle of world fame; a self-made man in every sense who pursued the American dream and lived it to the fullest while inspiring millions of young and not-so-young men around the world to be the very best they could be in life.

Anyone can use these exercises to transform themselves just like the great Atlas, and myself, into a powerful muscular he-man with his method of Isotonic muscle-building exercises. This book is more than bodybuilding, this book is designed to enhance your overall health, strength and lifestyle. This book will show you first-hand, by training you, motivating you, and teaching you how to build a magnetic personality.

You will increase your muscle size, strength and gain confidence. Charles Atlas has inspired millions of young men around the world to be the best they can be. This book contains the most efficient muscle-building exercise strategies which means less trial and error for you and faster gains. However, it does take some work, but with this book you will build more muscle and strength without ever going to a gym or lifting weights. **YOU ARE YOUR OWN GYM!**

Be Transformed

Marlon Birch

In Health and Strength

HOW TO BEGIN

POWER
ISOTONICS

----

01 WHAT IS POWER ISOTONICS

Power Isotonics.

Power Isotonics are full range Dynamic Self-Resistance exercises that goes through the full range of motion. Bicep curls where one group of muscles are supplying resistance to another group of muscles are termed dynamic self-resistance. This form of exercising was the mainstay for Atlas and the other greats used to develop their muscle mass. In truth, it is a method where one muscle group acts as resistance for another. These exercises may appear simple, but they can be very vigorous and taxing. However, it does take effort and concentration as one limb acts as resistance for another while going through the full range of motion.

Tension and Force.

How much tension to use? When starting off use a light tension until you become comfortable with applying resistance. Practice using a scale between 1-10. Ten being the hardest form of resistance and one being the lightest. Use a resistance of 5-7. Far too much tension or force will create tendon issues, please use a light to medium resistance (force) this will increase muscle size and strength gains just as weights or machines.

Frequency.

Self-Resistance exercises can be done on a daily basis. As much as twice or three times a day or more if you have the time. As stated above start off using relatively light to medium resistance that will allow you the trainee to complete 15-20 reps per set before the muscle begins to tire. Or 10-30 reps depending on the exercise and feel. Once you have mastered the exercise movement you can vary the resistance used, but do not use extreme resistance.

02 CHEST EXERCISES

It's important to hit the chest muscles from many angles as possible to coax and force development.. However, I learned that in order to really build a good chest it isn't one or two exercises it's a variety that will build the chest and increase its strength! So in truth the best thing to do is to divide the chest into sections.Upper Chest, Inner Chest, Lower Chest. Instead of looking at it as a whole because it isn't. You must treat the upper and lower chest as two separate entities for your chest building venture to be a success.

BASIC & STRETCH: Incline push-ups. Elbows in, hands-on two chairs works the lower chest really well. Along with help from the front portions of the shoulders and the triceps muscles.

STRETCH & CONTRACTED: Liederman Presses and Across the body presses really hit both elements in pre-stretching and increasing the peak contraction at the end of the movement. This position involves muscle-teamwork as well which will help the chest perform the movement. Help from the shoulders and triceps. Let's take a look at some muscle sculpting exercises.Development of the chest muscles was a priority of Atlas, here's a number of exercises to superbly develop and enhance that area.

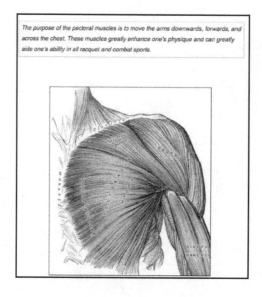

The purpose of the pectoral muscles is to move the arms downwards, forwards, and across the chest. These muscles greatly enhance one's physique and can greatly aide one's ability in all racquet and combat sports.

02 CHEST EXERCISES

Incline Pushups

This exercise is the Granddaddy of all upper-body exercises. This was his key upper-body exercise for the chest. It's the best upper-body builder and conditioner there is. This exercise is performed exactly as shown. Place your hands on two chairs that are 15 inches high, the higher you go the greater pre-stretch there is. At the bottom position to enhance muscle-building stimuli pause at the bottom for 2-3 seconds before reversing the movement. Perform 15-25 reps per set.

02 CHEST EXERCISES

Deep Breathing Exercise

This is the one exercise that should be done on a daily basis. If possible, try performing this movement outside in order to breathe in fresh air. This exercise will get the oxygen flowing through your body while expanding and adding strength to your rib cage and adding to the size of your chest. As shown place arms out to the side, inhale deeply then bring the arms forward while exhaling forcefully.

Repeat 20-30 times.

02 CHEST EXERCISES

Stiff Arm Pulldown

Begin with your hands placed level with your shoulders right hand over left. Start pushing with the right arm downwards while resisting with the left arm. While maintaining tension, lower the tension with the bottom arm just enough to allow movement of a full range of motion towards the thighs then reverse the direction by pushing up with the bottom hand while resisting with the top arm. Continue for 15-20 reps at 3 sets.

02   CHEST EXERCISES

Up and over dynamic Isometric pull

Grip the middle of each hand as shown. Pull outwards powerfully while raising the arms overhead, then behind the head. Maintaining the tension of the pull, then reverse the position while maintaining the tension back at the start position shown. Perform 3 sets of 20 reps per set.

02 CHEST EXERCISES

Across the body chest press

Here is an excellent exercise for the chest. Place your right fist in your left hand at the level of you right hip elbows bent. Against resistance of the left arm press the right arm towards the left hip resisting with the left hand. Perform 3 sets at 15-20 reps.

Liederman press

This is an awesome building and shaping movement. Works the entire chest, lower, upper and middle chest as well as the shoulders and triceps musculature. Start off with the hands as shown at the right armpit. Press right palm against the left palm towards the left armpit. Pause for 1-2 seconds and press the arm back to the other armpit, pause again before repeating.

02 CHEST EXERCISES

Chest chair dips

In the position shown raise the body up and down as many times as you can in sets of 15-20 reps. This dipping stimulates the lower chest muscles to its maximum.

03 SHOULDER EXERCISES

Everyone wants a pair of strong well-developed shoulder muscles. However, the shoulder is broken down into three heads, (front, side, and rear) We will show the trainee how to develop all three heads equally to increase muscle size, shape and added strength.

Now it's been said that the lateral (side) will only be activated with lateral movements, but both forward and side resisted raises will stimulate the two heads. The reason? One works with the other and they are intertwined with each other. The shoulder routines are packed with strength building and muscle pumping exercises that will create more width and roundness with efficient muscle stimulating exercises. So Let's take a closer look.

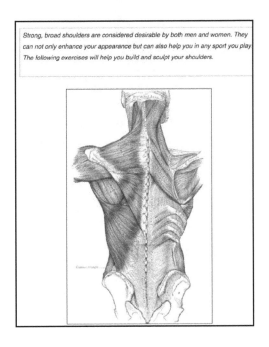

Strong, broad shoulders are considered desirable by both men and women. They can not only enhance your appearance but can also help you in any sport you play. The following exercises will help you build and sculpt your shoulders.

---

03 SHOULDER EXERCISES

Isometric Forward press

This is an isometric motion meaning (no isotonic-full-range movement takes place). Go into the position as shown, allow your arm to go slightly backwards now press the arm forward as you resist with the left arm. The arm will come forward for a few inches, but the key is to hold it. Hold for a count of 20-30 seconds at 3 sets each arm. **PLEASE DO NOT HOLD YOUR BREATH!**

03 SHOULDER EXERCISES

Across the body pulls

Bring the right elbow across the chest and grasp the left elbow with a firm grip. Slowly force the right elbow across the body towards the right hip resisting with the left hand. This exercise adds strength and development to the rear shoulder muscles and upper back. Perform 3 sets of 15-20 reps.

03 SHOULDER EXERCISES

Forward Raises

Grasp the right hand with the left in front of the body as shown. Gradually raise the arm forward against the resistance of the other hand. Perform 3 sets of 12-15 reps. Then switch arms and continue. This works the front shoulder muscles.

----

03 SHOULDER EXERCISES

Side lateral raises

Grasp the left arm that is across the body as in the picture. Now raise the arm out-wards towards the side contracted position resisting with the right arm. Perform 15 reps then switch arms, 3 sets each side.

03 SHOULDER EXERCISES

Reverse Upright Row

Place your arm behind your back as shown, hold onto the wrist with the other hand lean forward a-little and pull the right arm upwards while resisting with the right hand. Perform 3 sets of 15 reps when fatigue switch arms and continue.

This works the mid-back, upper traps and rear delts.

04 NECK EXERCISES

The neck muscles and upper trap muscles are the most important muscles in the body apart from the lower back. The neck is very important and supports the weight of your head that's 8-10 pounds. All the neck exercises increase the strength, size and shape to the neck. As we say in the fitness world, alignment starts at the top! A well-rounded neck/upper traps routine will enhance one's posture and maintain balance for the head.

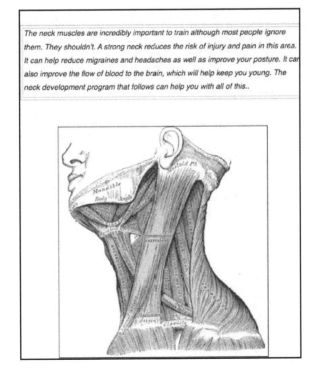

The neck muscles are incredibly important to train although most people ignore them. They shouldn't. A strong neck reduces the risk of injury and pain in this area. It can help reduce migraines and headaches as well as improve your posture. It can also improve the flow of blood to the brain, which will help keep you young. The neck development program that follows can help you with all of this..

04 NECK EXERCISES

Forward Neck Press

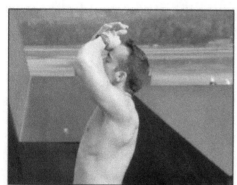

With your head tilted back place your hand on your forehead. Now slowly press your head forward and resist the movement slightly with light tension towards your upper chest. Always use a light tension to the neck. As your strength increases use a little more force but not too much tension. **Breathe Normal**.

04 NECK EXERCISES

Side to side neck press

Bend your head as close as you can to the shoulder as shown. Place the left hand on the left side of the head and press the head to the opposite shoulder while resisting with the hand. Followed by placing the right hand on the right side and press the head back to the starting position as before. Dual action left then right. Remember use a light tension and once the neck becomes more conditioned and stronger increase the tension.

---

04 NECK EXERCISES

Rear neck press

This movement is the opposite of the first movement. Place one hand behind your head and tuck the chin on the upper chest as shown. Now press the head against the hand while resisting with the hand until you're looking straight up. Use a light tension at the beginning and increase the tension to medium as you get stronger and more conditioned. Perform 3 sets of 15-20 reps.

05 UPPER-BACK EXERCISES

The structures of the upper back is quite powerful every point needs to be very carefully targeted. Basic Synergy Muscle Teamwork, works well here. Thigh Rows, Resisted Pull-downs or Three Chair Dips, these exercises are major corner-stone exercises that target the powerful upper back muscles.

The upper back is very complex and house loads of different muscles like larger areas of the back the lats, upper neck and mid back muscles. This will hit the smaller muscles as well. The best way to start is to break things down into sections to see where what is targeting to really realize what you're doing and how to effectively target that large mass of muscle more efficiently.

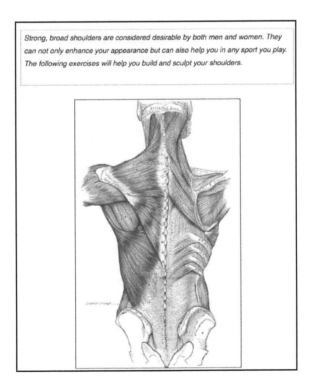

Strong, broad shoulders are considered desirable by both men and women. They can not only enhance your appearance but can also help you in any sport you play. The following exercises will help you build and sculpt your shoulders.

05   UPPER-BACK EXERCISES

Thigh rows

These are perfect for targeting the upper and lower lat muscles as well as the lower back. Apart from that there's Resisted Across the Body Rows that targets the lats fully from top to bottom. These exercises are under continuous tension within the range of pull. However, with the Thigh Rows resistance drops off a bit at the top position, but by all means a highly effective exercise. Interlock the fingers behind the knee as shown with right leg.

With both arms pull the thigh upwards towards the chest while resisting with the leg. This exercise widens the upper back, works the mid-back and stimulates the biceps as well. Work one side fully then switch to the other side. If balance is an issue perform the exercise seated.

05 UPPER-BACK EXERCISES

Upper-back kick out

Assume the squatting position above with hands on floor, then quickly kick the legs out as shown in the picture above. Then quickly reverse the position to the squatting position. Perform 3 sets of 20 plus reps. This will condition the upper-back as well as conditioning the entire system.

05   LOWER-BACK EXERCISES

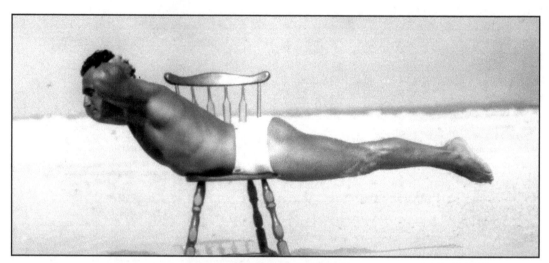

Lower-back extensions

While lying on a chair or stool or simply flat on the floor, raise your upper body upwards until you feel a strong contraction in the lower-back. This is a favorite exercise of mine that stabilize the entire upper-body, plus builds a brace of muscle around the entire spinal structure. Perform 3 sets of 15-25 reps

05 UPPER-BACK EXERCISES

Across the body rows

Bring your right arm across the body pre-stretching the mid-back, grasp the wrist with the left hand. Slowly pull the arm across the body toward the right arm-pit against the resistance supplied by the left hand. Repeat the movement then switch arms. This adds thickens to the mid back and lats, along with the rear part of the shoulders. Perform 3 sets of 12-15 reps.

05 UPPER-BACK EXERCISES

Three chair dips

As shown place each hand at least 15-16 inches apart, or shoulder width. Lower the body between the chairs pause one second and reverse the movement to the starting position. This is an awesome upper back widener

---

05 UPPER-BACK EXERCISES

Pulldowns

With the arms overhead place your left hand on top of the right fist as shown. Pull down with the left hand resisting with the right, once at finished position press the right hand up resisting with the left hand for the desired reps. Then, switch arms.

This works the entire upper back, biceps and shoulders muscles.

05   UPPER-BACK EXERCISES

Stiff arm pulldowns

Grasp the left hand with the right as in the picture. Gradually pull the arm down-wards while resisting with the bottom arm. At finished position, Repeat by pressing the bottom arm up again by resisting against the top hand. Resisting in both directions for reps, then switch. Fantastic Upper and mid back strengthener.

06 BICEPS EXERCISES

OK, I've made a few changes to the original resisted curl to make it far more effective in building strength shape and muscle faster than before. At the very beginning while performing the original resisted curl gains were good, but not great. Once I learned how to make the exercise harder and more efficient that's when my biceps and forearms really started to grow and take shape. It's all about efficiency in effort by changing this around to make it work better for you.

People are always looking at anyone that walk up that look a little fit or muscular, and what's the first thing they look at? The biceps and forearms. That's the first thing they see really. I've noticed it and all the people I've talked to about it have said so as well. It also helps when there's veins all around. What I've realized is that while I was developing or trying to develop my biceps and forearms my forearms got wider and was impressive when flexed, but my biceps looked narrow and when flexed flat looking. My biceps weren't as impressive hanging at my sides.

It wasn't wide enough. So, I paid attention to the exercises that would make a difference and one of the lessons I learned is to change the way I did the regular Atlas curls at different angles and hand positioning. This made a difference with increasing the diameter of my biceps. Now when I stood, I looked at my biceps in the mirror it's the inner part of the bicep that gives that width! Height is another thing that the long head on the outside and the muscle that's under the bicep needs to be developed as well..the brachialis.

Anyway, let's focus on what I did then we'll break things down with my special biceps and triceps section. So here we go: Let's look at the muscle sculpting exercises.

06 BICEPS EXERCISES

06 BICEPS EXERCISES

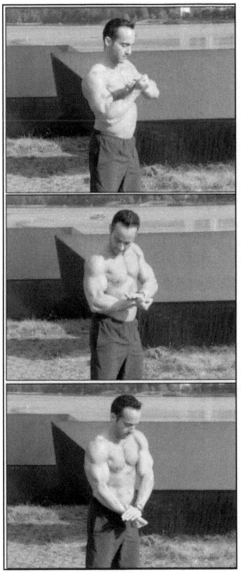

Bicep curl

Grasp your right fist with the left hand. Pull the right arm upward towards the shoulder while resisting with the left hand. At the shoulder, reverse the exercise by pushing the left arm downwards resisting with the right. Continue for reps then switch arms.

06 BICEPS EXERCISES

Behind the back curls

With your right arm behind your back, place your left hand on the wrist of the right, lean forward until you feel a stretch in the biceps (front of arm). Curl the right arm towards the right arm pit then reverse the movement for 10-15 reps at 3 sets then switch arms.

06 BICEPS EXERCISES

Hammer curls

Another great Bicep/Forearm combo. Place the wrists as shown in the picture above. Now pull with the right hand or bottom hand upwards to the chest while resisting with the top hand. At upper chest level reverse the exercise by pressing the top wrist down and resisting with the bottom wrist. Repeat for reps then switch arms.

06 BICEPS EXERCISES

Concentration curls

This is a great bicep finisher move. Peak contraction to hit that long head again. As pictured in start position hold on to the right wrist with left hand and pull the right arm towards the face while resisting with the left hand. Now reverse the exercise by pushing the left arm down and resisting with the right. Complete your reps then switch arms and repeat movement.

07 TRICEP EXERCISES

Tricep pressdown

The triceps long head is the largest part of the triceps musculature. It's responsible for the most triceps size. The triceps are broken into three muscle-heads. Lateral (outer head), Long Head (inside muscle), and the Middle or medial head. (middle muscle). The triceps are easily developed due to dips, push-ups and a variety of self resistance type exercises. The self resistance exercises are geared to stimulate the triceps throughout the full range motion through three separate ranges of push.

07 TRICEP EXERCISES

Forward lateral press

Place the left fist in the right hand. Now push the left hand forward while resisting with the right hand. At the finished position reverse the movement by pulling the right hand towards you while resisting with the left.

07 TRICEP EXERCISES

Over head tricep press

Make a fist with both hands place it behind your neck. Now press the bottom fist upward while resisting with the top fist. At the top reverse the exercise by pushing downwards with the top fist while resisting with the bottom fist. Use a light to moderate tension due to the triceps tendons being quite sensitive at that position.

07 TRICEP EXERCISES

Decline tricep extension

Place your feet on a chair or box as shown in the picture. Place your hands and lower-arms on the floor and slowly press the arm straight out with a slight bend to the elbows. This exercise stimulates the outer head (lateral) muscle of the triceps.

08 FOREARM EXERCISES

Powerful forearms just like upper arms command respect! This muscle needs to be balanced with the upper arm. The last thing you want are forearms that look weak with powerful upper-arms. So, here's a number of exercises to increase the gripping strength, and overall musculature of the lower arm, connective tissues of the wrists and increases and strengthens the grip.

08 FOREARM EXERCISES

Wrist curls palms down

As pictured extend the left wrist downwards and place the right hand pressed against the back of the hand. Now flex the left wrist upwards while resisting with the right hand. Perform 3 sets 12-20 reps then switch hands and repeat.

08 FOREARM EXERCISES

Wrist up palm curls

As pictured extend the right wrist backwards placing the left hand pressed against. Now flex the right wrist upwards while resisting with the left hand. Practice till tired or desired reps are done then switch hands and repeat. Reps can be 3 sets at 15 reps each.

----

09 THIGH EXERCISES

Ok let's focus on the powerful thighs and hamstring developing exercises. Developing strength and power is what every athlete as well as every person wants. How do we achieve that? Let's start from the very top: One Legged Squats the King of All Lower-Body exercises stimulate everything! Thighs, hips, hamstrings, inner thighs and glutes (butt). Followed by Leg extensions, and leg curls we are talking maximum efficiency. Strength-building-multi-joint exercises that stimulate the important hips, thighs and glutes is all we need.
So, let us get started.

The hip and thigh muscles are the largest in the body. Athletic, muscular legs are not only attractive and vital to playing sports, but they are also one of the keys to staying young. "Healthy legs act like a heart for the lower body", someone once said, and they're right. If you want to stay young, you need to keep that blood pumping. Healthy legs will keep you young, strong and vital for life.

---

09 THIGH EXERCISES

Few exercises are as impressive as a properly conducted one-leg-squat. Some of the best athletes and strength coaches in the world are unable to perform a single rep of this advanced exercise, let alone a full set of them. In time though, with solid practice, you will develop an awesome pair of muscular thighs, hamstrings and inner thighs to go along with it. Stand with your knees slightly bent and your arms outstretched to balance.

Lift one leg off the ground and place it as far-out in front of you as possible while keeping it straight. (don't worry you will get better in time). Then, slowly lower yourself as far as possible on your balancing leg. When your hamstrings touch your calves (or as far as you can perform this exercise at first), push back up with the supporting leg to the start position and repeat. If your balance isn't tip top perform the exercise holding on to a chair with a free hand for support.

09 THIGH EXERCISES

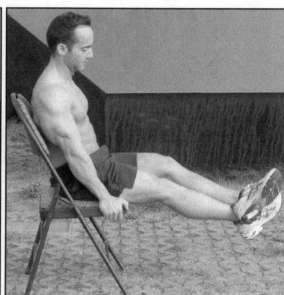

Leg extensions

While seated on a chair, box or stool, place the right leg over the left as shown in the picture, and extend the left leg outwards resisting with the right. At the top reverse the movement by pulling down the right while resisting with the left.

09 THIGH EXERCISES

Balanced squats

Perform this squatting movement-on the ball of your feet support yourself with your hands lower yourself to the position shown then raise up to the starting position. Fantastic for overall thigh development as well as the calves. To increase and produce greater growth hormone production combine this movement with leg extensions to increase time under-load.

09 THIGH EXERCISES

Crossed feet squats

Another excellent exercise for the overall thigh and hamstrings. Start off as shown in the bottom position with feet crossed. Slowly under control push yourself to the finished position. NO BOUNCING! One second pause then reverse the movement to the starting position. This exercise may be difficult at first but keep practicing and as night follows day it gets easier.

09 HAMSTRING EXERCISES

Leg curls

While on the stomach on the floor place the left leg over the right as shown, Now pull the right leg upwards towards you while resisting with the left leg. Pull on the up phase only. Repeat for reps then switch legs.

10 CALVE EXERCISES

Calf growth due to the dense layers of the muscles itself is quite stubborn! So my results within this department wasn't the best. However, I've learned a few things. In order for my calves to improve various steps had to be taken into consideration. I did loads of high reps daily but lost the true meaning of building muscle within this area. In order to add muscle onto those it's best to really focus on how you're doing the exercises and what rep range you're using for ultimate muscle building stimulation, which I'll explain in a moment.
Here, they are:

STRETCH: You achieve this position at the bottom of any calf exercise—calves stretched off a high block. It's important to get that stretch to force the calves to contract at it's maximum!

HIGH REPS: As I've said earlier the calf is one dense muscle. The majority of these calf fibers are endurance oriented fibers because they are used daily. You contract these muscles all day by walking so they need to be taxed a certain way. The best way to target the calves are with reps that hit the range between 30 to 35 reps per set.

Tension times are increased for your straight sets of calf work and should be about one minute or more to efficiently hit the dense fibers effectively. As with any muscle group you must pay attention to the feel and focus on the muscle at hand. It is important to avoid bouncing and fast reps. Rep speed is also important. Three seconds up and the same speed for the down portion is about right.

However, feel is the most important element here. Another key to maximizing calf development and to increase the stress is to maintain the tension on the calf muscles.

10 CALVE EXERCISES

By not coming all the way up to full contraction this maintains constant tension on the muscle and increases blood blockage. This will indeed increase growth stimulation, capillary development and muscle overload and what about the bottom range? This is just as important. It's important to get a max stretch at the bottom of the movement. This really pre-stretches the muscles to fire more efficiently due to the powerful stretch that loosens up the fibers, which produces additional growth.

More Calf-Growing Details: Now guys I don't have genetically superior calve development. Well not yet anyway. I'm still working on it. After my experiment I added a component that was never done for my calves effectively, but last year my calves got even better than the year before with less work per set. They looked almost two inches bigger. It didn't make sense really. So I introduced a number of techniques and stress methods into my calve workouts for the first time to see the effects of it all. Lo and behold my calves responded far better to the stress methods.

My calves looked much better with more size, shape and increased vascularity, naturally. I'm not blessed with inner-calf flare so seeing that the methods increased that fact I loved it to the max! By doubling up on the key contracted point of the movement with mini reps at the end of my full reps made the set far more intense. That's only one method I did. You will see more in later chapters in the routine sections.

10 CALVE EXERCISES

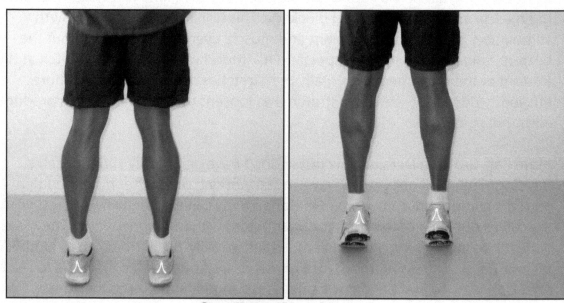

Standing calve raises

This exercise can be done on the stairs or block. Start as shown and go up and down contracting the calves at the top of the movement. If on stairs, extend the heels as low as you can to really pre-stretch the calves, then press upwards into the contracted position.

10 CALVE EXERCISES

Slanted calve raises

Stand at least 30 inches away from the wall, or position yourself as shown, but make sure the calves are well stretched. Start off as shown in the picture start position. Press straight up on the toes then lower. This is as awesome calf stretch exercise. Perform this exercise until the calves are well tired. This stimulates the entire calf muscle.

11 ABDOMINAL EXERCISES

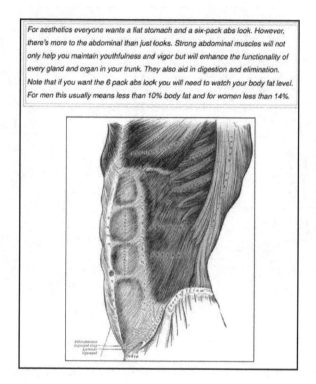

For aesthetics everyone wants a flat stomach and a six-pack abs look. However, there's more to the abdominal than just looks. Strong abdominal muscles will not only help you maintain youthfulness and vigor but will enhance the functionality of every gland and organ in your trunk. They also aid in digestion and elimination. Note that if you want the 6 pack abs look you will need to watch your body fat level. For men this usually means less than 10% body fat and for women less than 14%.

Abdominal muscles are endurance type fiber muscles. Very much like forearms and calve muscles they need longer tension times and high rep ranges to benefit from training. Muscle Makeup: The abdominal muscles are just that—muscles. It's one sheet of muscles with tendons dividing the muscles into blocks. So, it isn't upper and lower it's one sheet. Each is made up of the same types of fibers as your biceps, chest and back; however, as I mentioned, many of the fibers in the abs are more endurance oriented and require higher reps to reach full development.

The main abdominal muscle that one need to be concerned with, is the rectus abdominis (front area). This isn't a bunch of knotted muscles, as it appears to be, but rather a sheet-type muscle that runs from the bottom of your rib cage and attaches to your pelvis.

---

11 ABDOMINAL EXERCISES

As I've said earlier, the ripples are actually caused by tendons running horizontally and vertically. Throughout the entire length that cause the block type muscle separation you see. Hip Flexor Function: The hip flexors come into play on many ab exercises, such as reverse crunches. As you will soon see, the hip flexors are important contributors when you exercise the rectus abdominis. Upper and lower separation. Like I said, there's no real separation on upper and lower abs.

Studies indicate that the upper rectus abdominis can work somewhat independently of the lower part of the muscle, as it does when you perform crunches or abdominal sit-ups (feet extended not anchored) when you work the lower-portion, your upper rectus always comes into play, as in reverse crunches or across the body crunches. Therefore, you should always work the lower area first, which brings both upper and lower sections into play. If you isolate the upper part first, you fatigue that area and make your lower ab work much less effective—in much the same way that working forearms before biceps can limit your biceps efforts.

For example, if you do crunches first and, then reverse crunches, which works your upper rectus will be so fatigued from the crunches that it will cause you to fail on the reverse crunches long before you fatigue your lower abs—it's one reason so many trainees lack lower ab delineation: They work lower abs last or do only crunches in their ab program. So here's just a few exercises that gets the job done. It works the muscles in union in order to get the best of both worlds.

----

11 ABDOMINAL EXERCISES

Side plank

This exercise works the external oblique muscles which are on both sides of the abdominal wall. Perform the exercise as pictured, it is a simple exercise to master. Perform 20-25 reps at 3-4 sets per side.

11 ABDOMINAL EXERCISES

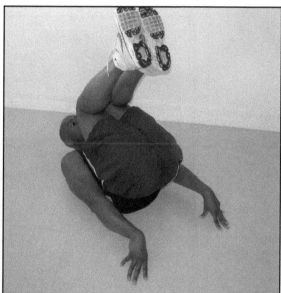

Reverse crunches

Start as shown in the start position picture. Then roll the hip as you bring the knees into the chest lower to second picture shown for 20-25 reps at 3-4 sets.

11 ABDOMINAL EXERCISES

Leg raises

Extend your legs straight out on the floor then proceed by lifting them up towards the upper-body then lower the legs back down again. Perform 20-25 reps at 3-4 sets each

SPLIT ROUTINE
WORKOUTS

---

12 SPLIT ROUTINE WORKOUTS PHASE ONE
WORKOUT ONE (CHEST, NECK, BACK, BICEPS, CALVES)

Perform these exercises at 15-20 reps for 3 sets each. Rest time between sets 10-20 seconds. Workout one and workout two are to be alternated for 6 days straight 2 weeks.

----

12 SPLIT ROUTINE WORKOUTS PHASE ONE
WORKOUT ONE (CHEST, NECK, BACK, BICEPS, CALVES)

12 SPLIT ROUTINE WORKOUTS PHASE ONE
WORKOUT ONE (CHEST, NECK, BACK, BICEPS, CALVES)

12 SPLIT ROUTINE WORKOUTS PHASE ONE
WORKOUT TWO (NECK, SHOULDERS, TRICEPS, LEGS, ABS FOREARMS)

Perform these exercises at 10-15 reps for 3 sets each. Resting 10-15 seconds between sets.

12 SPLIT ROUTINE WORKOUTS PHASE ONE
WORKOUT TWO (NECK, SHOULDERS, TRICEPS, LEGS, ABS FOREARMS)

---

12 SPLIT ROUTINE WORKOUTS PHASE ONE
WORKOUT TWO (NECK, SHOULDERS, TRICEPS, LEGS, ABS FOREARMS)

---

12 SPLIT ROUTINE WORKOUTS PHASE TWO
WORKOUT ONE (CHEST, CALVES, BACK, BICEPS)

Perform workout one and two alternating days 6 days straight for 2 weeks. Reps 20 at 2 sets per exercise.

----

12 SPLIT ROUTINE WORKOUTS PHASE Two
WORKOUT ONE (CHEST, CALVES, BACK, BICEPS)

12 SPLIT ROUTINE WORKOUTS PHASE Two
WORKOUT ONE (CHEST, CALVES, BACK, BICEPS)

12 SPLIT ROUTINE WORKOUTS PHASE Two
WORKOUT TWO (CHEST, SHOULDERS, LEGS, NECK, FOREARMS, ABS)

12 SPLIT ROUTINE WORKOUTS PHASE TWO
WORKOUT TWO (CHEST, SHOULDERS, LEGS, NECK, FOREARMS, ABS)

----

12 SPLIT ROUTINE WORKOUTS PHASE TWO
WORKOUT TWO (CHEST, SHOULDERS, LEGS, NECK, FOREARMS, ABS)

12 SPLIT ROUTINE WORKOUTS PHASE TWO
WORKOUT TWO (CHEST, SHOULDERS, LEGS, NECK, FOREARMS, ABS)

---

12 SPLIT ROUTINE WORKOUTS PHASE TWO
WORKOUT TWO (CHEST, SHOULDERS, LEGS, NECK, FOREARMS, ABS)

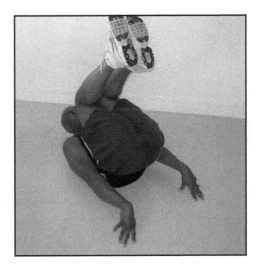

FULL BODY

WORKOUT I

12 FULL BODY WORKOUTS PHASE THREE
WEEK ONE

Perform this routine 6 days straight 3 sets resistance exercises 10-12 reps. Body-weight exercises 20 reps rest time between sets 10-20 seconds.

12 FULL BODY WORKOUTS PHASE THREE
WEEK ONE

12 FULL BODY WORKOUTS PHASE THREE
WEEK ONE

----

12 FULL BODY WORKOUTS PHASE THREE
WEEK ONE

---

12 FULL BODY WORKOUTS PHASE THREE
WEEK ONE

12 FULL BODY WORKOUTS PHASE THREE
WEEK ONE

----

12 FULL BODY WORKOUTS PHASE THREE
WEEK ONE

FULL BODY

WORKOUT II

12 FULL BODY WORKOUTS PHASE FOUR
WEEK TWO

Perform this routine 6 days straight 2 sets resistance exercises 20 reps. Bodyweight exercises 20-30 reps rest time between sets 20 seconds.

12 FULL BODY WORKOUTS PHASE FOUR
WEEK TWO

----

12 FULL BODY WORKOUTS PHASE FOUR
WEEK TWO

12 FULL BODY WORKOUTS PHASE FOUR
WEEK TWO

12 FULL BODY WORKOUTS PHASE FOUR
WEEK TWO

12 FULL BODY WORKOUTS PHASE FOUR
WEEK TWO

12 FULL BODY WORKOUTS PHASE FOUR
WEEK TWO

12 FULL BODY WORKOUTS PHASE FOUR
WEEK TWO

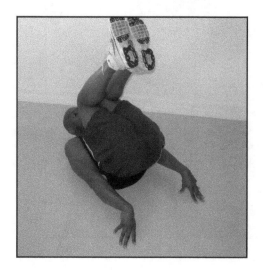

Upper Body
Lower Body
Workouts

----

13 UPPER BODY/LOWER BODY WORKOUTS PHASE FIVE
WORKOUT GROUP ONE

Perform all four exercises shown one after the other without resting until the entire round is completed for three rounds (sets). Then, rest for 10-20 seconds before beginning the other group of four exercises. Perform 15 reps each exercise at 3 sets each round.

13 UPPER BODY/LOWER BODY WORKOUTS PHASE FIVE
WORKOUT GROUP TWO

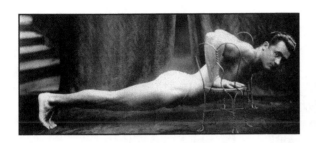

13 UPPER BODY/LOWER BODY WORKOUTS PHASE FIVE
WORKOUT GROUP THREE

13 UPPER BODY/LOWER BODY WORKOUTS PHASE FIVE
WORKOUT GROUP FOUR

13 UPPER BODY/LOWER BODY WORKOUTS PHASE FIVE
WORKOUT GROUP FIVE

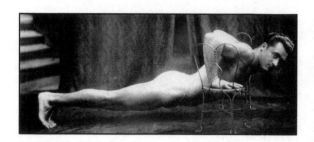

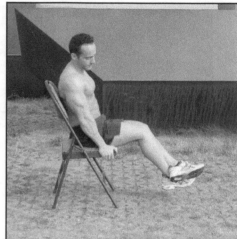

13 UPPER BODY/LOWER BODY WORKOUTS PHASE FIVE
WORKOUT GROUP SIX

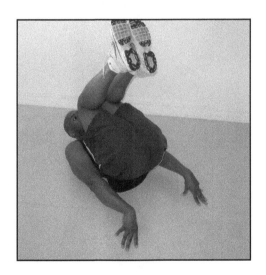

13 UPPER BODY/LOWER BODY WORKOUTS PHASE FIVE
WORKOUT GROUP SEVEN

----

13 UPPER BODY/LOWER BODY WORKOUTS PHASE FIVE
WORKOUT GROUP EIGHT

Acknowledgments

My greatest amount of gratitude goes out to my Grandparents for their support: Francis and Claris Birch (Grandparents), without them these books would have never been written. They are my greatest inspiration. My wife Kiri Birch for her never-ending support. My very good friend Robert, Daniel my Lawyer and Anand that have always stood at my side.

The appreciation you have given me throughout the years, I cannot repay. The appreciation I have for all of you who assured me I can do it throughout the years. I Thank You. Now, my never-ending motivation Dr. Desiree Charles for without their love, support, and positive outlook on life, they both pushed me forward and said.........KEEP MOVING FORWARD. Thank you all for all the support throughout the years.

P.S. Please contact me on your progress at skippymarl007@gmail.com or marlon@birchtreepublishing.com

Be Transformed

Marlon Birch
In Health and Strength

CPSIA information can be obtained
at www.ICGtesting.com
Printed in the USA
BVHW091808010222
627782BV00005B/220

9 781927 558591